Sojourner Truth
Path to G

By Peter Merchant

Illustrated by
Julia Denos

Ready-to-Read • Aladdin
New York London Toronto Sydney

**For Pocca, like Sojourner,
a loving defender of her cause,
faithful preacher, and beloved grandmother.
Thank you for your courage.
—J. D.**

ALADDIN PAPERBACKS
An imprint of Simon & Schuster Children's Publishing Division
1230 Avenue of the Americas, New York, NY 10020

Also available in an Aladdin Library edition.
Designed by Lisa Vega
The text of this book was set in Century Oldstyle BT.
Manufactured in the United States of America
First Aladdin Paperbacks edition January 2007
8 10 9
Library of Congress Cataloging-in-Publication Data
Merchant, Peter.
Sojourner Truth : path to glory / by Peter Merchant ; illustrated by Julia Denos.
—1st Aladdin Paperbacks ed.
p. cm.—(Ready-to-read)
1. Truth, Sojourner, d. 1883—Juvenile literature. 2. African-American abolitionists—Biography—Juvenile literature. 3. African-American women—Biography—Juvenile literature. 4. Abolitionists—United States—Biography—Juvenile literature. 5. Social reformers—United States—Biography—Juvenile literature. I. Denos, Julia, ill. II. Title.
E185.97.T8M47 2007
306.3'62092—dc22
[B]
2006025020
ISBN-13: 978-0-689-87207-5—ISBN-10: 0-689-87207-0 (pbk.)
ISBN-13: 978-0-689-87208-2—ISBN-10: 0-689-87208-9 (library binding)
0920 LAK

Chapter One
Birth of a Slave

Sojourner Truth was born a slave.

Being a slave means being owned by another person. Before the Civil War, it was legal for people to own African American slaves in the South. But slavery was also legal up North. Many slaves lived in New York State, and Sojourner Truth was one of them.

Sojourner Truth was the name she gave herself later in life. Her first name was Isabella Baumfree. No one knows exactly when she was born. Because she was born a slave, the child of parents who were slaves, her birth date was not written down. But it was probably before 1800.

From the time Isabella was just a baby, she slept on the floor of a cold, dark basement. Her life was hard.

When she was four years old, Isabella watched as her owner took her three-year-old sister and five-year-old brother away in a box and sold them to another slave owner.

By the time Isabella was five years old, she was already doing chores around her master's house. She was not allowed to go to school, and she was not taught how to read. She was forced to work.

When she was only nine years old, Isabella was taken away from her parents and sold to another slave owner, like her brother and sister had been.

Life away from her parents was terrible. Her new masters often beat her.

One year later she was sold once again, this time to an innkeeper.

Isabella worked hard, making beer and working in the garden, but she was still beaten.

Slaves were treated worse than animals.

After two years with the innkeeper, Isabella was sold to some very mean masters: John and Sally Dumont.

Isabella worked for Sally Dumont around the house in the morning. Then she went outside and worked for John in the fields through the afternoon. John praised Isabella for doing the work of many men, but he still beat her because his wife wanted him to. Sally hated Isabella and followed her around the house, yelling at her.

For sixteen years Isabella was a slave for the Dumonts. Then, in 1827, an amazing thing happened: All New York slaves born before 1800 were freed! That meant Isabella was free—for the first time in her entire life.

As a free woman, Isabella chose to live at the house of Maria and Isaac Van Wagenen, and work as their maid. The Van Wagenens were very different from the Dumonts. For one thing, they thought slavery was wrong. They believed that Isabella was a human being, not an object. They treated her kindly.

While she was working for the Van Wagenens, Isabella found something that changed her life: religion. She started praying and going to church. She became a Methodist.

During the 1800s Methodists believed in singing, shouting, and letting their feelings show in church. This religion was perfect for Isabella. She had a lot of feelings stored up inside her from all her years of being a slave. Now she could let those feelings out. She found comfort in the idea that God existed and that God cared about her.

Sometimes, while she was dusting or mopping or cooking, Isabella would start preaching. It didn't matter to her if anyone was listening—but one day the Van Wagenens were listening. They told Isabella she should be a preacher.

Isabella—a preacher? That was the craziest idea she had ever heard! She had spent most of her life as a slave, scrubbing floors and being mistreated by her masters. Most preachers were white men, and Isabella was a black woman. At that point in American history, a black woman had no power.

But even so, Isabella started picturing herself preaching to a large group of people. The more she thought about it, the more she liked it.

Chapter Two
Isabella the Preacher

In September of 1828 Isabella stepped onto a boat on the Hudson River.

She had decided to go to New York City to follow her dream of being a preacher. She was sailing with two Methodists named the Grears. The Grears wanted to help Isabella meet other Methodists in New York City.

The plan worked. As soon as she set foot in New York, Isabella met a nice Methodist family, the Latourettes (pronounced "La-tuh-rets").

James Latourette invited Isabella to move in with him and his family.

Isabella worked in their house as a maid, but she was also treated as a friend. The Latourettes invited her to go with them to "camp meetings" just outside of the city. Camp meetings were big outdoor Christian festivals. Many preachers would speak.

At one camp meeting, Isabella stood and started preaching. By this point, Isabella was a full-grown woman. She was nearly six feet tall, and she had a loud, booming voice. When she began preaching and singing, people listened.

This was the start of Isabella's life as a preacher. Isabella became very popular. Lots of people came to listen to her.

Many people were amazed by Isabella. Many white people still did not think that African Americans were human beings. However, when they heard Isabella speak, they changed their minds. With her powerful sermons, Isabella gave them proof that she was not just human, but a truly great human being.

Chapter Three
Sojourner Truth

June 1, 1843, was an important day for Isabella Baumfree. For one thing, it was an important Christian holiday called Pentecost. Pentecost is a day when some Christians hear a calling from the Holy Spirit of God to go and preach.

On this Pentecost, Isabella was called. She would leave New York. She would become a traveling preacher. She would change her name to Sojourner Truth.

Using the name Sojourner Truth was her way of showing the world exactly who she wanted to be. A sojourner is a traveler, a person who goes from place to place. The truth is what she always tried to tell. Sojourner Truth's mission in life would be to tell the truth, wherever she went.

On June 1, 1843, Sojourner Truth started her new life. She set off on foot as a traveling preacher with a new name. Carrying only as many things as would fit in a pillowcase, she left New York City and started walking east, toward Long Island.

She had almost no money—just one quarter—but Sojourner Truth believed that God would take care of her. She believed that kind people would let her live with them and give her food. And she was right. Everywhere she traveled, Sojourner Truth never went without food or shelter.

Her first stops were at many camp meetings in Brooklyn. There was a shortage of preachers at these meetings, so Sojourner Truth was always welcome. But she never stayed for long.

By September Sojourner Truth had walked more than one hundred miles through New England. The days became shorter and colder. She knew that soon it would snow, and she would have to make camp for the winter.

Sojourner Truth settled in the town of Northampton, Massachusetts. She had met a nice group of people who invited her to live and work with them in their big house. She accepted.

Sojourner's new home in Northampton was unlike anything she had ever seen. It was huge. Inside, a hundred people lived and worked together. During the day, they cooked and cleaned and farmed and made silk. In the evenings, they listened to invited guests speak. They talked about women's rights and slavery.

Slavery, in fact, was the main topic of discussion in Sojourner Truth's new home. Everyone there was against slavery, and their discussions had to do with putting an end to slavery. One of the most famous visiting speakers was a man named Frederick Douglass. Like Sojourner Truth, he was both a preacher and a former slave. Mostly, he preached against slavery.

Listening to Frederick Douglass speak gave Sojourner Truth an idea. What if she told the world the truth about her life as a slave? Douglass had written a book about being a slave. He sold it everywhere he went. What if she wrote a book about her life as a slave?

She decided to do it.

In 1845 Sojourner Truth started speaking at antislavery meetings. It was easy for her. She was already a great speaker, and her early life as a slave made her an expert on the subject.

Writing a book was harder. Sojourner had never learned how to read or write. She dictated her life story to a friend named Olive Gilbert. They called it *The Narrative of Sojourner Truth*.

A man named William Lloyd Garrison lent Sojourner Truth money to pay for the cost of printing the book. And in 1850 her book was ready for the world to see. Sojourner hoped that she could sell many copies so she could afford to keep doing what she wanted to do: go from one town to the next, speaking wherever people would listen.

Chapter Four:
A Star Is Born

In the spring of 1851 Sojourner took to the road again, with a suitcase full of her books. This time she traveled by train. One of her first stops was in Akron, Ohio. In the 1850s people all over America were arguing about women's rights and their right to vote. On May 28, the Ohio Women's Rights Convention was meeting in Akron's Stone Church.

Most of the women's rights leaders were white women like Amy Post, Lucy Coleman, and Frances Dana Gage. Sojourner Truth was different. As a former slave, she knew what it was like to have no rights at all. She brought something completely new to the white men and women at the Ohio Women's Rights Convention. When she stood up to speak, everyone gave her their full attention.

“I have as much muscle as a man,” she said. “I have plowed and reaped and husked and chopped and mowed, and who can do more than that?”

No one argued with her. They could see she was telling the truth.

But she wasn’t done.

She said, "How came Jesus into the world? Through God . . . and woman. Man, where is your part?"

In the Bible, Jesus was born because of God and the Virgin Mary. There was no man involved! She was trying to make a point.

Sojourner ended her speech with a warning to white men. She told them they better pay attention to African Americans and women, since they all wanted more power. Soon the white men would be in a "tight place . . . between a hawk and a buzzard."

This speech made Sojourner Truth a star. She gave the best reasons anyone had ever heard for why women should be allowed to vote. As a slave, she had done men's work. So why shouldn't she have the same rights as a man? As a speaker at this meeting, she had proven herself to be wise. Why shouldn't someone who was wise be allowed to vote?

Sojourner Truth offered solid proof that both women and African Americans were at least equal to white men.

Wherever she went, Sojourner Truth spoke about why she felt women should be able to vote. And at every meeting she sold her books. With every book she sold, she became a little more famous, and a few pennies richer.

When she spoke to mainly white audiences, she told them to end slavery. She spoke out against a new law called the Fugitive Slave Act. This law allowed Southern slave owners to capture slaves who had escaped to the North. Sometimes, Sojourner Truth argued with her audience.

In 1858 the nation was on the brink of civil war over the question of slavery. Sojourner Truth went to Indiana, where many people were proslavery. One such man got up and asked Sojourner Truth to prove she was a woman, and not a man. He was making fun of her.

Sojourner Truth knew exactly what to say. She told him that as a slave she had nursed many white babies—and she was sure that these babies had grown up to be better men than he was.

Moments such as this made Sojourner Truth very famous.

In 1863 Sojourner Truth became even more famous. The author Harriet Beecher Stowe wrote an article about her called "Sojourner Truth, the Libyan Sibyl." It was published in a magazine that all sorts of people read. Suddenly everyone around the country knew who she was.

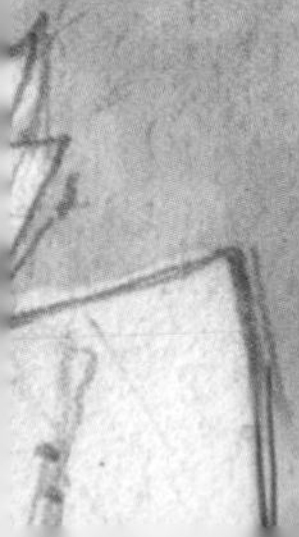

Stowe's article caused someone else to write an article about Sojourner Truth: the president of the Akron meeting, Frances Dana Gage. She wrote a story about Truth's famous speech at that meeting. In this story Gage claimed that Sojourner Truth repeated the phrase, "Ar'n't I a woman?" It's not likely that Sojourner Truth ever said this, but she became known for these words.

Sojourner Truth has meant many things to a lot of different people. For many, Sojourner Truth was an antislavery hero. For women, she was a women's rights leader. For others still, she was a great preacher who knew how to impress a crowd with her words.

What Sojourner Truth did with her life is incredible. Before she died in 1883, she kept doing great things. During the Civil War she was invited to the White House. She met the president, Abraham Lincoln. During and after the Civil War she helped freed slaves start new lives in Washington, D.C. She fought for their rights and showed them how to help themselves.

By her own example Sojourner Truth showed the world how someone born with nothing, not even freedom, can rise up to become very powerful, to help other people, and to make a difference in history.

Here is a time line of Sojourner Truth's life:

(Sojourner's early life is undocumented. The dates in bold have been suggested by historians.)

1798 Isabella Baumfree is born into slavery in New York state.

1802 Isabella's brother and sister are taken away by the master.

1807 Nine-year-old Isabella is sold to a new master for $100.

1810 Twelve-year-old Isabella is sold to the Dumont family.

1827 On July 4 the New York Emancipation Act is passed, freeing all slaves born before 1800. Isabella Baumfree is officially, legally a free woman.

1828 Isabella moves to New York City.

1843 On June 1 Isabella changes her name to Sojourner Truth. As Sojourner Truth, she becomes a traveling preacher. In November, Truth moves to Northampton, Massachusetts, and meets abolitionists such as Frederick Douglass.

1850 The Fugitive Slave Act passed into law, allowing Southern slave owners to hunt down slaves that have escaped to the North.

1851 Sojourner Truth publishes her book, *The Narrative of Sojourner Truth*. On May 28 Truth speaks at the Ohio Women's Rights Convention.

1852 Harriet Beecher Stowe's novel *Uncle Tom's Cabin* is published.

1857 Sojourner Truth moves to Battle Creek, Michigan.

1858 Truth is challenged in Indiana to prove her womanhood.

1861 The Civil War begins.

1863 President Lincoln delivers the Emancipation Proclamation, making slavery illegal in America. Harriet Beecher Stowe publishes a famous article on Sojourner Truth titled "Sojourner Truth, the Libyan Sibyl."

1865 The Civil War ends.

1883 Sojourner Truth dies in Battle Creek, Michigan.